01 July 2019

Happy 4th Birthday, Henry

Great Aunt Theresa &
Great Uncle Tony

How the
PEANUT DUDE
FOUND
Gratitude

Charleston, SC

by Chris Bible
a.k.a. *The Peanut Dude*

Published by Chris Bible and Ginger Bible (*a.k.a.* Mom), Love you.

Special Thanks to my Best Friend & Business Partner Hudsen

Illustrations by Lucy Elliott
Graphic Design by Berge Design
Art Collaboration with Chris Bible

One Dollar from each book sold will be used to purchase items for donation to MUSC Children's Hospital Child Life Services. For more information on how to help visit *www.musckids.org/childlife*.

ISBN: 0692297146
ISBN 13: 978-0-692-29714-8

Printed in the USA by Signature Book Printing, www.sbpbooks.com

DEDICATION

For My Grandmother Bible

&

Grandmother Starr

Margaret Ruth Bible
6.17.1931 – 7.22.2013

Delores Neil Starr
9.13.1934 – 8.21.2013

The Peanut Dude awoke
one early morning in his bed.
With thoughts he couldn't explain
bouncing around in his head.

He was joyful, smiling,
happy as could be.
But nothing had changed
from last night to this morning, you see?

The Peanut Dude was so happy,
with tons of joy inside.
The Peanut Dude was so thankful,
tears of joy fell from his eyes.

Excited, filled with energy,

The Peanut Dude jumped from his bed.

He ran to his family

and here is what he said:

"Hey y'all, I want to tell you

about this dream that I had.

And tell you about this feeling

of Gratitude I now have."

"In my dream I was sad, wishing I had more.

When I met this wise man named Whispering Larry,

who asked me to tell him

all the things I was thankful for."

"It took me a minute

because I was feeling down.

But suddenly, in my mind,

happy thoughts began to bounce around."

"My mind was no longer focused

on what I did not have.

Instead, my mind was focused

on all that I DID HAVE!"

The Peanut Dude shouted,

"This is a new way of thinking for me!

Whispering Larry, I want to thank you

for the wisdom you've shared with me!"

"Because of you, I can finally see

that the key to my happiness

is being thankful for:

All that I am. All that I have. And all that I can be!"

Whispering Larry simply smiled and said,

"That feeling you feel is the feeling of Gratitude.

And Gratitude is simply being thankful

for all that's around us and all that we have."

"Thank you," I said, as Whispering Larry

slowly walked away.

"My dream was over and I, The Peanut Dude,

awoke to see a brand new day!"

"That's awesome, that's great!"
The Peanut Dude's family exclaimed.
Then his brother shouted,
"Hey, I know a game we can play!"

"Let's go through the alphabet
from the letters A to Z.
And tell each other what we are thankful for
that starts with each letter, you see?"

Wow! It was awesome!

And cool as could be!

The Peanut Dude's family was playing

The Gratitude Game from A to Z.

Sounds of joy and laughter

could be heard all around.

As each spoke of the new Gratitude

they had found.

"I am Grateful for Air!"

"I am Grateful for Bees!"

"I am Grateful for Chocolate!"

"I am Grateful for Dreams!"

On and on they played…

until ending on letter Z.

And from that day forward

The Peanut Dude and his family

were all truly HAPPY!

THE END

GRATITUDE

As Defined By Merriam-Webster

a feeling of appreciation or thanks

GRATITUDE *as Described by* **Others**:

"Gratitude is not only the greatest of virtues, but the parent of all others." ~Cicero

"He is a wise man who does not grieve for the things which he has not, but rejoices for those which he has." ~Epictetus

"What you focus on expands, and when you focus on the goodness in your life, you create more of it. Opportunities, relationships, even money flowed my way when I learned to be grateful no matter what happened in my life." ~Oprah Winfrey

"Everybody can be great. Because anybody can serve. You don't have to have a college degree to serve. You don't have to make your subject and your verb agree to serve. You don't have to know about Plato and Aristotle to serve. You don't have to know Einstein's theory of relativity to serve. You don't have to know the second theory of thermodynamics to serve. You only need a heart full of grace. A soul generated by love." ~Martin Luther King Jr.

"Be the Change you wish to see in the World." ~Gandhi

"Gratitude: Actively Being Aware and Actively Acknowledging The Hearts Ever-Present Inner-Joy." ~Chris Bible

"When I started counting my Blessings, My whole life turned around." ~Willie Nelson

"Things turn out best for people who make the best of the way things turn out."
~John Wooden

"Gratitude is the Hearts Memory." ~French Proverb

GRATITUDE *as Described by* **Me:**

_____

- -

_____

- -

_____

- -

_____

- -

_____

- -

_____

GRATITUDE GAME

**How to Play The Peanut Dude Gratitude Game —
From A to Z**

The Gratitude Game can be played alone or with multiple players.

Object of the Game:

To enjoy and expand the feeling of gratitude as you go through the alphabet from the letters A to Z. Saying out loud what it is you are grateful for, starting with each corresponding letter of the Alphabet.

For example:

Player one would say out loud "I am Grateful for Air," player two would say out loud "I am Grateful for Baseball" and so on. You play until ending on the letter Z.

My Ever-Growing Gratitude List — From A to Z

A -

B -

C -

D -

E -

F -

G -

H -

I

J

K

L

M

N

O

P

Q

R

S

T

U

V

W

X

Y

Z

visit our website
www.PeanutDude.com